Herman Parish

Amelia Bedelia, Bookworm

Pictures by Lynn Sweat

SCHOLASTIC INC.

New York Toronto London Auckland Sydney
Mexico City New Delhi Hong Kong Buenos Aires

No part of this publication may be reproduced in whole or in part,
or stored in a retrieval system, or transmitted in any form or by any means,
electronic, mechanical, photocopying, recording, or otherwise, without written permission
of the publisher. For information regarding permission, write to Greenwillow Books,
an imprint of HarperCollins Publishers, 1350 Avenue of the Americas, New York, NY 10019.

ISBN 0-439-57660-1

Text copyright © 2003 by Herman S. Parish III. Illustrations copyright © 2003 by Lynn Sweat.
All rights reserved. Published by Scholastic Inc., 557 Broadway, New York, NY 10012,
by arrangement with Greenwillow Books, an imprint of HarperCollins Publishers.
SCHOLASTIC and associated logos are trademarks and/or registered trademarks of Scholastic Inc.

23 22   18 19/0

Printed in the U.S.A.   40

First Scholastic printing, September 2004

Watercolors and a black pen were used for the full-color art.

The text type is Times.

For Anne Bezverkov,
who loved books
—H. P.

For Elynor
—L. S.

"**H**i, Mrs. Page," said Amelia Bedelia.

"How is the world's best librarian?"

"Amelia Bedelia," said Mrs. Page.

"Am I glad to see you."

"I give up," said Amelia Bedelia.

"Are you glad to see me?"

"Of course I am," said Mrs. Page.

"I am just frazzled today."

"What's wrong?" said Amelia Bedelia.

"It is my boss," said Mrs. Page.

"The head librarian is stopping by.

When it comes to libraries and books,

she knows it all."

"She sounds very smart,"

said Amelia Bedelia.

"Did she invent books?"

"Almost," said Mrs. Page.

"She has been around forever."

"Don't worry," said Amelia Bedelia.

"She'll love your library. The children do."

"Thank you," said Mrs. Page.

"I just wish her visit could be special."

"I will help," said Amelia Bedelia.

"First, I must return some books."

Mrs. Page was astonished.

"What have you done to them?"

"Remember?" said Amelia Bedelia.

"You said these books needed jackets.

So I made a jacket for each one."

"This book got a sweater,"

said Mrs. Page.

"Sure," said Amelia Bedelia.

"It is about the North Pole.

It gets very cold there."

"Now I have seen everything,"

said Mrs. Page.

"This is one book

you *can* judge by its cover."

"Excuse me," said Mark.

"May I check out this book?"

"Certainly," said Mrs. Page.

"Here is your book, Mark."

"Yippee!" said Amelia Bedelia.

"Free bookmarks for everyone."

"Bookmarks?" said Mrs. Page.

"Who is giving out bookmarks?"

"You are," said a girl.

"You gave that boy a bookmark."

"I did not," said Mrs. Page.

"I said 'Here is your book, *Mark*,'
because that boy is named Mark."

"My name is Danny," said Danny.

"Too bad," said the girl.

"If you were named Mark,

you could have a bookmark."

"That is not fair!" said Danny.

"Amelia Bedelia," said Mrs. Page,

"see what you have started?"

"I am sorry," said Amelia Bedelia.

Mrs. Page got paper, scissors, and pens.

"Children, Amelia Bedelia will help

each one of you to make a bookmark."

"What about Mark?" said Amelia Bedelia.

"Don't forget him," said Mrs. Page.

"Make him a bookmark, too.

Just be as quiet as you can.

I want to hear a pin drop."

"Okay," said Amelia Bedelia.

She threw her pen on the floor.

CLICK

"How was that?" said Amelia Bedelia.

"Do you want to hear my pen drop again?"

Mrs. Page shook her head and walked away.

Amelia Bedelia got right to work.

She drew a picture of Mark

on his bookmark.

She made each bookmark special.

"Next!" said Amelia Bedelia.

"What is your name?"

"My name is Ralph," the next boy said.

"But I don't need a bookmark.

 I need help with my school report."

"What is it about?" said Amelia Bedelia.

"Dinosaurs," he said. "You know,

tyrannosaurus, allosaurus,

ste . . . stego . . ."

"Stego Saurus?" said Amelia Bedelia.

"That's the one," said Ralph.

"It figures," said Amelia Bedelia.

"If your last name is Saurus,

you are probably a dinosaur."

"Excuse me," said a girl.

"I need some help, too.

 I am looking for a thesaurus."

"The Saurus?" said Amelia Bedelia.

"What kind of dinosaur is that?"

"I'm not sure," said the girl.

"Is a thesaurus a dinosaur?

 My teacher said

 I needed one to do my report."

"Gee," said Amelia Bedelia,

"you are way too late.

Every Saurus died

millions of years ago."

"What am I going to do now?"

said the girl.

"Let's make a bookmark for you,"

said Amelia Bedelia.

"What is your name?"

"My name is Lisa," she said.

"But I don't need a bookmark,

because Sam ate my book."

"Yipes!" said Amelia Bedelia.

"Is Sam okay? Where is he?"

"Sam is fine," said Lisa.

Lisa pointed out the window.

"Sam is cute," she said,

"but he chews up everything."

"Whew," said Amelia Bedelia.

"I was worried about Sam."

"I am worried, too," said Lisa.

"Mrs. Page will be mad

that her book got wrecked."

"I see," said Amelia Bedelia.

"Let's go talk with her."

"Mrs. Page," said Amelia Bedelia,

"Lisa has a book checked out."

Mrs. Page looked up the title.

"Here it is," said Mrs. Page.

"*How to Train Your Dog.*"

"That's the book," said Lisa.

"But Sam got it."

Mrs. Page corrected Lisa.

"You mean Sam *has* it.

Did he enjoy it?"

"He sure did," said Amelia Bedelia.

"Sam devoured it."

"Wonderful!" said Mrs. Page.

"We librarians love that."

"You do?" said Amelia Bedelia.

"Oh, yes," said Mrs. Page.

"But it breaks my heart

if a book is abused or lost.

A missing book must be replaced."

"Of course," said Amelia Bedelia.

"Rules are rules," said Mrs. Page.

"You have to go by the book."

"Right," said Amelia Bedelia.

"We have to go buy the book."

"You see," said Mrs. Page,

"lots of people depend on us,

especially those

who cannot visit the library.

I mean, take our bookmobile . . ."

An assistant interrupted her.

"Oh, Mrs. Page, the head librarian

will be here in twenty minutes."

"Goodness," said Mrs. Page.

She ran off to get ready.

"Lisa," said Amelia Bedelia,

"Mrs. Page told us what to do.

We need to go buy the book.

And we can take the bookmobile."

"May I come, too?" said Lisa.

"Sure," said Amelia Bedelia.

"Just ask your mother first."

"Here she comes," said Lisa.

"She was teaching an art class."

Lisa's mom gave permission.

"May I ask a favor?"

said Amelia Bedelia.

"These children may need help

with bookmarks and reports."

"I'd be glad to help," Lisa's mom said.

"Thanks," said Amelia Bedelia.

"We'll be right back."

"I love this bookmobile,"

said Lisa.

"Me, too," said Amelia Bedelia.

"Let's pretend we have checked out

all these books for ourselves."

"Lucky us," said Lisa.

"It was nice of Mrs. Page

to loan us the bookmobile,"

said Lisa.

"It was all her idea,"

said Amelia Bedelia.

"Stay here, Sam," said Lisa.

"And stay away from the books."

"I found the book," said Amelia Bedelia.

"Good work," said Lisa.

"Guess what I found? A thesaurus."

"Where is it?" asked Amelia Bedelia.

"Right behind you," said Lisa.

"Run! Hide!" said Amelia Bedelia.

Lisa laughed out loud.

"Come back," she said.

"A thesaurus is not

a dinosaur, after all."

"Jeepers," said Amelia Bedelia.

"Look at all these words.

I can find just the right one to use."

A man walked up to them.

"I am the manager of this store.

What is all the ruckus about?"

"Ruckus?" said Amelia Bedelia.

"I like that word. Let's look it up.

I would love to use it in a story."

"Ah-hah," said the manager.

"Follow me. You are late."

"I am?" said Amelia Bedelia.

He led them straight to the

children's section of the bookstore.

He said, "I like your costume.

I have never met a storyteller

who dresses like a housekeeper."

Lisa laughed.

Amelia Bedelia did not laugh.

She did not want to disappoint

the manager or the children.

Amelia Bedelia told a terrific story

about dinosaurs attacking the library.

Mrs. Page, the brave librarian,

saved every book from being chomped.

"All in all, it was quite a ruckus,"

said Amelia Bedelia.

"You are great,"

said the children.

"You are talented,"

said the manager.

"You are in trouble,"

said a police officer.

"What's wrong?" said the manager.

"There must be some mistake."

"There sure is," said the officer.

"This lady took that bookmobile."

"I sure did," said Amelia Bedelia.

"Mrs. Page told me to."

"Don't worry,"

said the officer.

"They won't throw

the book at you."

"I hope not,"

said Amelia Bedelia.

"I just bought it."

The officer smiled.

"I will trust you to drive

back to the library,"

she said.

They returned the bookmobile.

"I wonder if Mrs. Page is upset,"

said Amelia Bedelia.

"Why would she be upset?"

said Lisa. "We bought the book."

Mrs. Page was not smiling.

Neither was the woman

standing beside her.

"I owe you an apology,"

said Amelia Bedelia.

"Sam had ruined a book.

You said, 'Go buy the book.'

So we borrowed the bookmobile

and bought the book."

"Oh, dear," said Mrs. Page.

"What happened to our book?

 Were the pages torn or just dog-eared?"

"Ask Sam," said Amelia Bedelia.

"He's still digesting it."

"Hey, there! Welcome back,"

said Lisa's mom.

"I know some other creatures

who would like to say hello."

ARRRRGH!

"I am the word-eating Thesaurus!

If you need a better word,

look inside me!"

"I am the Flying Periodical.

I buzz by every week!"

"I am the Giant Prehistoric Bookworm!

If I had a nose, it would be in a book."

The woman who had not smiled

was now laughing.

"You are all amazing," she said.

"I have been the head librarian

for twenty years,

but I have never seen children

have such fun with books."

"Lisa's mom helped everyone,"

said Amelia Bedelia.

"So you are the head librarian.

I have heard all about you.

You are the know-it-all

who has been around forever."

Mrs. Page was about to faint.

The woman laughed and said,

"I guess I am a dinosaur."

"Let's check," said Amelia Bedelia.

"Is your last name Saurus?"

"No," she said, "it is Cramer."

"I am sorry," said Amelia Bedelia.

"You cannot be a dinosaur."

"What a relief," said Mrs. Cramer.

"There is a big parade next week,"

Mrs. Cramer said.

"Would you all march for the library?"

On the day of the parade

Amelia Bedelia stopped by the library.

"Amelia Bedelia," said Mrs. Page,

"I *am* glad to see you.

Come see what Mark made for you."

RETURN

Amelia Bedelia looked up

at the ceiling.

"Is that a mobile?"

"It is a *book* mobile," said Mrs. Page.

"How sweet," said Amelia Bedelia.

"Just remember," said Mrs. Page.

"You can borrow the books

but not the bookmobile."

They laughed.

Then they went out together

to watch the parade.